THE HUMAN WAR

Snowbooks

2 4 6 8 10 9 7 5 3 1

Copyright © Noah Cicero 2003

First published by Fugue State Press, New York 2003
This edition published by Snowbooks, London, 2007

Book design by James Bridle

Proudly published in Great Britain by
Snowbooks Ltd.
120 Pentonville Road
London N1 9JN
www.snowbooks.com

A CIP catalogue record for this book is available
from the British Library

ISBN 9781905005468

THE HUMAN WAR
NOAH CICERO

snowbooks

LONDON

ABOUT THE AUTHOR

Noah Cicero lives in Ohio. His short stories have appeared in many magazines and on the Internet. He also writes social commentary in collaboration with Oma Mullins. This is his first book.

www.myspace.com/noahcicero

CONTENTS

THE HUMAN WAR

Two hours till war.

It's six o'clock. Bush said at eight, people must die.

I'm going to Kendra's.

I'll hide out there. Are the terrorists coming?

I'm standing in my living room at my parents' house. My dad is sitting on his special seat, my mom on the couch, and my brother on the reclining chair.

They're watching the news.

The news isn't saying much.

My brother says he's going to fight on the side of Iraq.

My dad tells him to watch what he says. My brother doesn't care, he rambles on about money and oil.

My mother sits there quiet. Then she bitches about Bush.

My dad doesn't know what to make of it. He's confused, but it's entertaining, and that's why he's watching.

War is entertaining.

I can't take their insanity any more, so I leave.

Each minute, the war gets closer.

I grab my keys, and put on my beret.

I leave.

I head out to my car. Turn it on and drive away.

A guy is on the radio talking about the war.

Speculating.

Speculating.

Speculating.

He says in less than two hours, we shall fight to preserve freedom.

Freedom.

America wants to give another country freedom.

That doesn't sound that bad, or does it.

I hope the terrorists don't attack. I read in the paper a couple of days ago that the terrorists would fuck up America if we attacked Iraq. I hope they were just trying to scare us.

They probably won't attack Youngstown Ohio.

There is nothing here of any importance. It will probably be New York again.

I went to New York City and nobody spoke English there. I felt as if I wasn't even in America.

Like I was on some strange island full of all the nationalities of the earth. Not America.

But what is America.

I've seen a lot of America. Oregon, California, New York City, Nebraska, Arizona, Florida, South Carolina, and the New England area. In all those places I found completely different people. People that had no relation to each other.

They all lived under freedom though.

None of them cared though.

They just wanted their homes and their families to be safe.

That's all.

The guy talks on the radio about war.

I listen and don't know whether to care or not.

Should I care, or not care, that's the question.

I'm on a lot of medication. It's hard to care; I'm numb all the time.

Every day has the same weather when you're on medication.

The sun is neither out nor hid away by clouds.

It just doesn't matter.

I feel weird.

There is a lot of darkness this evening.

War.

I remember when I was little watching the Gulf War on television. I wasn't scared, I was excited by it.

Now I'm scared.

I get to Kendra's.

I knock on the door of the trailer. Kendra opens the door.

There she is.

Kendra and all the history we've had together.

Kendra and I have known each other since we were fifteen. We are now both twenty-two. We've dated off and on since then. We have said I love you to each other many times over the course of seven years.

We were engaged last year for ten months. Then I had a threesome and told her.

I told her because I wanted to hurt her.

We go into the living room. She sits down on the couch, and I sit on the floor.

"What's up?" Kendra said.

"I've been walking the world alone."

"I walk the world alone too, but I like it that way."

"Why, doesn't it get to you?" I said.

"No, it doesn't. I can do my own thing all the time. No one is bothering me; no one is fucking with my shit. Who needs people, when you have yourself."

"You remain alone because you don't like people judging you."

"I know, I hate to have people thinking about me. I always think they're thinking bad about me," Kendra said.

4

"People think you're great."

"Yeah, but I don't believe them."

We sit in silence for a second.

"Turn on the war," I said.

"Fuck no, I don't care."

"You don't care?"

"Why should I care, it doesn't have anything to do with me."

"Because it's interesting."

"It's not interesting, it's fucked up. I don't have any time for war, I have things to do."

"Like what?" I said.

"Paint my bathroom, and make curtains."

"You're right, you don't have time for the war."

"I know. War is absurd. Human beings shooting at each other. That doesn't make any sense," Kendra said.

"Nothing makes sense."

"Nothing?"

"Nothing. I thought America was civilized."

"We're not, honey," Kendra said.

"I don't wanna live in an uncivilized nation."

"You have to, for me, I need you."

"You need me, why. I don't do anything for you, and I piss you off most of the time."

"Because you're the only person I can really talk to."

"I talk pretty well to you too," I said.

"You believe in the war, don't you?"

"No, don't accuse me of that."

"No, you're lying, you love Bush."

"I fucking hate Bush, you insane?"

"You want people to die, don't you?" Kendra said.

"No, leave me alone."

"You want world domination, I know you do."

"I don't know what I want, but I don't want that."

"You're cute," Kendra said politely.

"Thanks."

"Last night I cried."

"Why?"

"The terrorists are coming to get me. They're going to put smallpox in the air, I know it. We'll all be dead in a week, and Jesus will come back," Kendra said.

"Jesus won't come back, and you won't die in a week."

"Jesus will come back and send Bush to hell for everyone to see."

"That would be nice," I said.

"Jesus doesn't like wars. He said to walk the extra mile."

"Bush doesn't care about that verse."

"He should, he says he's Christian."

"He's Christian for votes," I said.

"I'm going to kill him."

"You are."

"Yes."

"How?"

"I'm going to shoot a missile at the White House while he's sleeping in there all snug in his bed," Kendra said.

"Where are you going to get a missile."

"I'll find one, it can't be that hard."

"You should do it then, it would be good for your mental health."

"Yeah, it would release a lot of pent-up aggression," Kendra said.

"What are you going to do after you kill the President?"

"I'm going out to get drunk and celebrate."

"Good idea."

"Then I'll go to college to become a doctor."

"I thought you hated college."

"I guess you're right, I guess I'll stick to being a pizza delivery girl," Kendra said.

"Yeah, you are really good at it. I don't see why you should stop now."

"I know, I am good at it," Kendra said.

Absurdity.

"I don't want to be an American any more," I said.

"Leave then."

"Where can I go, I have no money, and no passport."

"Go to Mexico."

"I went there once, I got robbed," I said.

"Go nowhere then."

"How will I get there."

"By train."

"That's too expensive."

"Drive your car then."

"I have no insurance."

"Reject the absurd, and kill yourself," Kendra said.

"I'm afraid of death."

"Don't be afraid, Jesus saves."

"I don't believe in Jesus."

"No one does."

"Can America save me?"

"Only you can save yourself."

"I have no interest in being saved," I said.

"That might be the cause of your problems."

"I don't have problems."

"You have only yourself."

"I don't want myself," I said.

"No one does."

"There's a war."

"I don't care."

"No one does."

"What if America loses," Kendra said.

"Then the troops go home, and some don't."

"Then mommies cry."

"A lot more Iraqi mothers will cry."

"Yeah, but they don't matter."

"Why don't they matter?" I said.

"They aren't Americans, they're evil."

"What if they aren't evil?"

"If they aren't evil, why are we killing them?"

"Money."

"Someone will lose their existence for money?"

"Yes."

"I would never give up my existence for money," Kendra said.

"I wouldn't lose my existence for anything, except freedom."

"We already have freedom."

"Then we don't need to lose our existence."

"As a child, I never thought of war."

"War is for old people with money," I said.

"War is fought by young scared boys with low self-esteem."

"They chose to fight."

"Then we can't blame them," Kendra said.

"Who can we blame?"

"No one, I guess. I'm tired of this," Kendra said.

"What?"

"America and its civilization."

"A lot of people are weary of it."

"I'm tired."

"But no one is listening."

"I am the voice crying in the wilderness," Kendra said.

"But no one hears."

"You hear, don't you?"

"No."

"When I'm alone, I cry."

"And still no one hears."

"I want my tears to be seen by America, I want my tears on public television."

"America doesn't want your tears," I said.

"What does it want?"

"Blood."

"I have only tears to give."

"America wants war, it wants humans dead."

"I'm human."

"They want you dead," I said.

"Why would a human want to kill another human?"

"Power, silly."

"Power?"

"Yes, power."

"I have no power."

"No one does."

"I don't know what I would do if I had power."

"You'd misuse it," I said.

"I probably would."

"Everybody does."

"Is there no way we can stop this war?"

"It's impossible."

"Existence is impossible."

"Existence is war."

"I don't want to fight any more."

"You have to fight."

"I don't want to," Kendra said.

"No one does."

I looked at Kendra's face, it was beautiful.

There was pain in it.

She was beat down by this world.

I forgave her for being mad.

When I first met her, she was innocent. Now she's scarred and putrid. She is in a constant struggle for survival. But she goes on, she fights even though she doesn't want to.

I love to listen to her talk.

I'm heartbroken.

The bombs will soon drop.

Bush will be happy.

Kendra lay there, smoking. I stared at her. I loved her for that moment. She was so worried.

I reached out my hand and petted Kendra's face.

She purred like a kitten.

I imagined people dying. I saw parents crying, and little children without legs.

I didn't want to be an American any longer.

I want to be in Mexico drinking cerveza in a whorehouse. I want to smoke some meth and forget I ever existed.

I am never going to forgive America for this.

I thought this was a democracy.

Plato didn't believe in democracy.

Little children will watch this on television and wonder. They will get no real answers though; no one cares about real answers.

I thought the world was changing for the better.

I thought the hippies changed things.

Bush grew up in the sixties, why isn't he a hippy.

People change when they grow up.

They change for the worse.

They start worrying about money. Money becomes an all-consuming thought. Then they die.

I have no interest in dying.

But I have to. I have to care one day about things that don't matter to me.

I look at Kendra and think, I used to love her.

But I don't any more. But I tell her I love you, I tell her so many things.

She's monogamous to me, but I'm not to her.

But I still feel like I'm taking care of her. She knows

I date other people, but she puts up with it. She's so weak and fragile. I don't know what keeps her alive.

There is so much pain.

Absurdity.

Kendra crawls next to me. She wraps her body around mine. I hold her tight to me. Then I kiss her on the eyelids.

"I love you," she said.

"I love you too," I said.

I don't know why I said that. I didn't mean it.

I said it because I had to.

I say a lot of things because I have to.

I live a useless existence.

Do I love Kendra? Most likely no. I love no one. I walk the world alone.

I'm not fit for human consumption.

I used to be able to love. But I can't any more.

It's too hard. And I especially can't love while a war is on.

I want to love Kendra, but it's destroyed now since I've cheated.

And I like promiscuous sex too much.

It would be nice to hold the same person on a regular basis, but it gets boring. I grow weary of their bodies.

I'm a hard man to please.

I don't stay pleased for long.

Who am I, I ask myself.

Perhaps I'll never know.

I never know why I'm incapable of love.

Love is for mediocre people.

Intelligent people can't love.

We know too much about the madness.

Love is madness.

All human interaction is madness.

I never wanted to be a human.

This is not my fault.

The war is not my fault.

Every day I look at myself.

And I amaze myself.

At the things I do because of jealousy, the gain of power, and insecurity.

I don't recognize myself.

But there I am.

A monster.

An animal.

A monkey.

A human.

An American.

I never asked to be any of those things, I'd much rather be a dolphin or a butterfly. It would even be better to have been a cat.

I've punched so many time clocks.

And I've never been paid enough.

And I've never worked hard enough.

I'm not very responsible.

I don't really care about anything.

I never could find a reason to.

Or maybe I don't have the energy.

There better be a God. Someone needs to answer for this.

I need answers.

I need to understand my suffering.

And my happiness.

Why the world is absurd.

I've read a million books. And I don't think it has made my life better.

Maybe worse.

I cry.

The last winter was cold. It snowed almost every day.

I almost killed myself last winter.

I quit my job and ran away to New York City in December. I spent five hundred dollars in three days on strippers, beer, and poetry.

When I got home, I had no money. I had to buy Christmas presents with my parents' money.

I almost killed myself.

Please pity me.

It feels good to be pitied.

Absurdity.

I cried so many times in the winter.

But it didn't solve anything.
All my problems were still there.
They weren't big problems. But they were big to me.
I hate when people belittle each other's problems.
Problems are proportional to the person's brain they involve.
Someday I'll walk free again.
I'll walk in the desert of Arizona, smiling, with a bottle of cold water.
I'll laugh at these days.
Too bad that the people who will die in this war will still be dead.
I'll be alive.
And I'll go on for them.
I'll walk to the bottom of the Grand Canyon. I'll stand there like I'm in heaven. I'll be strong and powerful standing there with my feet in the Colorado River.
But they'll still be dead.
I have to go on.
I have to fight the good fight.
Absurdity.
Civilization was started in Mesopotamia.
Which is in Iraq.
This is where civilization has led us.
To technological war.
People will die.
I've never met them.

But I'm sure.

They had hopes.

Moms.

Dads.

Brothers.

Sisters.

They had people who loved them.

But they must die.

Because they follow orders from an asshole.

An asshole is a person who orders other people to kill other people.

Bush could be an asshole.

In the Old Testament God said, "Eye for an eye."

Jesus said turn the other cheek.

But Jesus no longer matters.

Especially to people who say they believe in him.

Christian Republicans love war.

They love money too.

They hate homosexuals.

And young girls who get abortions because they have no money to raise their children.

I don't know God.

I don't know what he wants.

They say he left a book explaining his likes and dislikes.

But it's too full of contradictions, and it lacks historical proof.

For me to take it seriously.

I grew up in the information age.

Science is my God.

I was taught only science could save me from the horrors of this world.

Not some mystical God.

I believe that there are ghosts.

But I don't know what that means.

I don't believe there are absolute truths.

Perhaps I don't even care about truth.

It's not like knowing the truth changes anything.

Money changes things.

And I don't have any money.

So I can't change anything.

I've been broke for three months now.

My parents give me five dollars a day to buy cigarettes and get coffee.

But I just got my income tax check back.

I got two hundred and seventy dollars.

Tonight I'm going to spend some.

That's my plan.

I'll escape from this war with money.

Money can save me from suffering.

My mother makes sixty thousand a year.

She still bitches about money.

If you gave her a million dollars, it still wouldn't be enough.

Nothing is enough for her.

And most other people.

I watch the people of the world.

They're dissatisfied.

Nothing is enough for them.

They have no peace.

They are constantly disgruntled.

I want to pet their faces, and tell them it will be all right.

But I know it will not help.

Existence.

No matter where you are.

It's hard.

Humans are an unhappy animal.

They live long lives with memories.

Jobs.

Religions.

Choices.

Families.

And never any answers.

Humans seek answers constantly.

But they know there are none.

The universe is answerless.

People are victims of their psychologies.

They can never escape the truth that their mind has made for them.

The people of the world are shattering under the immense power of civilization.

Absurdity.

"Kendra touch my penis," I said to her calmly.

She reaches her little hand in my boxers and fondles my penis.

"Touch my cunt," Kendra said politely.

I reach my big hand in her underwear. I begin rubbing her clitoris.

We both make noises.

I place my mouth to hers and kiss softly.

I put my other hand in the back of her pants and touch her buttocks.

She has a beautiful body.

I love touching her.

She is so soft.

I pull off her shirt.

Revealing her young firm breasts concealed within a bra.

I kiss the tops of her breasts.

Then her tummy.

Then I go back to kissing her lips.

She is still fondling my penis.

I'm still rubbing her clitoris.

Her vagina slowly becomes wet.

I plunge my fingers in.

She makes louder noises.

I love to hear a woman's soft voice make animal
noises.

Her eyes close.

She takes off her bra.

I take off my shirt.

She lies on top of me.

Her naked chest is petal-like against my chest.

We kiss like maniacs.

Pulling hair.

Rolling around on the floor.

I put her nipple in my mouth.

And suck with tender care.

Her vagina becomes more wet.

She loves to have her nipples sucked.

I take off her pants.

I kiss her thighs.

And rub my hands up and down them.

I take off my pants.

All the clothes left on are our underwear.

I pull hers off.

She pulls mine off.

We stand before each other naked.

I jam my penis into her vagina.

We do it missionary.

Her eyes remain closed.

I'm in love with her for that moment.

I go back and forth.

Noises are made.

The world doesn't exist.

Suffering doesn't exist.

There are no problems during sex.

I tell her to get on top of me.

We disconnect and she gets on top.

She puts me back in.

She goes up and down.

"People are going to die in a little bit and we're fucking," I said.

"What else can we do?"

"I don't know, it just feels like there must be something we should be doing."

"All we can do is fuck."

"But we're having so much pleasure, and people are going to be suffering so intensely in just a little bit."

"Listen Mark, there's nothing we can do. This war doesn't have anything to do with us. We're peasants, we don't matter," Kendra said.

"But I'm human, and I'm affected by this war."

"You're not affected, you mean nothing, you are shit in the big picture. We are all shit."

"I'm tired of being shit," I said.

"Get used to it."

"Why did my parents bring me into this world."

"Because women have a baby fetish," Kendra said.

"Women only have babies because they want attention."

"People love attention."

"Sex is the ultimate act of getting attention."

"That's why I have it."

"I know," I said.

"You know me too well, I can't love you."

"It's funner to love someone who really doesn't know you."

"I know you like a brother," Kendra said.

"I know, it isn't fun like it used to be."

"It used to be so fun, but now, we sit around like we're brother and sister watching television. The only difference is that we have sex."

"You're so good at fucking, I can't resist," I said.

"You're good too."

"Thank you."

"I love fucking you."

"I love fucking you too, I feel like I love you when we fuck."

"Me too."

"We've been fucking for seven years, will this ever stop?" I said.

"I know I can't go on with my life because I keep fucking you."

"Who cares about going on with one's life, this is all life is."

"Life isn't much."

"No it isn't," I said.

"Once upon a time we were children Mark, we were little and we played games, and smiled. Now look at us, the only time we can smile is when we're fucking."

"It's a sad state we're in."

"I want more from life, I want to live my dreams."

"How come you can't?"

"I can't leave the house, and I don't have any dreams."

"Everyone dreams."

"I don't."

"You should," I said.

"What could I be, a fireman, a rock star, what possibly could I be?"

"A painter, a writer, something, you just have to do something, you have to get motivated."

"I'm tired of trying to be motivated. Too much has happened to me to ever get motivated again," Kendra said.

"What has happened?"

"Well, first when I was a little girl someone decided to molest me repeatedly, then my father beat me constantly, and he never spoke to me. My Elektra complex is all fucked up," Kendra said angrily.

"I know, a lot has happened to you. But you have to go on, you have to keep trying."

"I don't want to try any more, I'm done trying. I work at Pizza Hut, that's my life now, pizza."

"You have such a beautiful personality, you could be a star."

"I can't be anything, what for, it's not like it will really matter. Someday I'll die, and hopefully there's a heaven, and that's all I can hope for now."

"There's so much more Kendra."

"There's only me and my madness."

"I worry about you, I worry that one day I'll come over and you'll be dead cos you've killed yourself, or you'll be in the mental ward."

"I'm fine, I can operate in the real world. I can work, I can function."

"I know, you function well."

"I'm worried about you, you don't function at all," Kendra said.

"You're right, I don't."

"You don't go to work, you cry all the time, and you're constantly having a panic attack. You're trapped in this world of shit, and I don't know if you'll ever get out of it. You used to be so full of hope and vigor, now you're like a lost man wandering alone in the desert."

"I am."

"Yes, you are, you're lost. You're so smart and powerful, but you're just wasting it. See I don't have a chance, but you do, don't waste it Mark, take advantage of your life, I know you could do anything if you just tried."

"I'm just in a slump right now, someday I'll get better."

"I know, you're just having a couple bad months."

"I'm going to take advantage of my life, I'm going to live it out to the end. When I die, people will admire and be jealous of my existence, and they will wonder how I did it all, how I lived such an exciting life."

"I know, you have it in you."

"Someday we won't know each other Kendra," I said sadly.

"I know, someday you'll move and never come back. You're not the kind of person to live in Ohio forever."

"It's not that I dislike Ohio, I just like other places better."

"Someday you'll be happy Mark, someday life will mean something to you."

"But you, what about you. You need to try to live again, you need to make something of your life," I said.

"I have all I need, I have this trailer, and I make enough money to keep it. So what does it matter. I have everything I need."

"But you don't make enough money to go on vacation, or save up."

"I don't worry about that, my dad will give me money if I need it."

"I guess you're right about that."

During this whole conversation we remain having sex.

I flip her over.

Then I did her doggy-style.

The war was on.

I looked at her and thought about how doomed she was.

How she was destroyed.

I shed a tear as I fucked her.

For her.

I pulled out and had an orgasm onto her back.

I stared at it.

It was powerful lying there.

She turned around and kissed me on the lips.

Then she stood up and went to the bathroom to wipe it off.

I sat there happy.

The war would soon start.

This is my existence.

This is who I am, and what I do.

I don't know if I like it, or even care for it.

But I do it.

I go on having sex, and drinking not caring if I live or die.

I don't think I'm mentally healthy.

But I don't care any more.

I've been suffering from depression since I was in ninth grade.

Since then I've been tormented.

Since then I've not wanted to be myself.

Kendra came back into the room and lay next to me.

We lit cigarettes.

There was love between us.

But I had cheated on her.

And she could never trust me again.

Therefore our love was destroyed.

I didn't care.

I don't think she did either.

We were just two humans looking for an escape.

That's all.

We were alone.

And tired.

"I don't feel right," Kendra said.

"How do you feel?"

"I don't know, I don't feel human."

"I feel like that a lot of the time. Like I'm not part of the human race, I'm something else, something alone and mad," I said.

"I feel angry."

"You don't act it."

"But I am, I'm so angry. I'm so tired."

"Don't worry, life will get better."

"Perhaps," Kendra said.

Absurdity.

"You kiss other girls, don't you?" Kendra said.

"You're on a need to know basis, we aren't going out."

"I know you, and I can't help but feel jealousy."

"You went out on a date the other day and told me about it. What was that?"

"I told you, I thought about you the whole time."

"Don't think about me the whole time, live your life. We don't love each other any more, we can never be again," I said.

"But, I love you."

"You don't love me, you love the memories you have of me. All we do together is have sex, we give each other pleasure to each other's genitals, that's what we do, and that's all."

"But you mean so much more."

"I don't mean shit."

"I know, you don't. I don't even think about you when you aren't around."

"I don't think about you when you're not around either," I said.

We finished smoking our cigarettes, and then held each other.

We lay there silent with our eyes closed.

I thought about the night ahead of me.

I have to go to Denny's and read for a little bit.

Then to the strip joint. Then to the bar for crapie-okie.

I don't know what will happen tonight.

I hope something happens.

I stand up and put my clothes on.

She lies there quiet staring at the television.

"Where are you going tonight?" Kendra said.

"I'm going to Denny's to read, then to the bar for crapieokie."

"You have fun."

"I will."

"Don't kiss any girls," Kendra said.

"I won't."

I kissed her on the lips and left.

I got into my car.

The radio was talking about the war.

There was useless speculating going on.

I don't know why I fucked Kendra.

I don't even know why I went over there.

I should just leave her alone.

But I can't.

There's something beautiful about her that I need.

Something my heart cries out for.

She could always make me laugh. Most women don't make me laugh.

I've known her for so long.

It's hard to live without her.

She is such a comfort to me in this time of crisis.

Since September Eleventh we've been in a crisis.

My father's generation had to fear the communists.

Now we fear Arabs.

Most likely when the Arab problem disappears, America will find someone new to fear and fight with.

It's so childish to fight.

When I was in school I fought a lot. They kicked me out of school.

People go to jail for killing people.

But a soldier becomes a hero.

I don't understand that.

I don't understand at all what America is doing.

And what Iraq is doing.

I don't understand at all.

I feel very alone.

I will walk this world alone, not understanding anything.

One hour till war.

I get to Denny's.

I go inside and see the glory of Denny's.

It's a shitty Denny's. It hasn't been refurbished

for years. It's probably one of the worst Denny's in America.

I sit down at the counter.

I start reading Proust while I wait for someone to get me coffee.

A waitress named Cindy comes over.

She's about thirty.

She's white trash.

She's missing teeth.

"How are you doing today Mark?"

"Good, how are you?"

"Oh fine, coffee?"

"Yeah."

She goes over and pours me a cup of coffee and puts it down in front of me.

I put two Sweet and Lows in it. And stir.

Steam is coming up from the warm coffee.

I take a sip. It's still too hot to drink.

I go back to reading.

I love reading.

It's the only thing that keeps me together.

I need books.

I need those dead man's lines.

I need their truth.

I like writers that write of necessity.

Writers that wrote because they had to.

Who were compelled to express.

They were driven by one thing only, and that was the written word.

I see books as the purest representations of an era.

When anthropologists a thousand years from now need to understand the psychology of the people of that time, they will look at their books. Not their bridges, computers, and skyscrapers.

There is an older black man sitting a couple of seats away from me at the counter. He suddenly says to me, "Civilization."

I look up from my book and reply, "Huh."

"Civilization."

"What about it?"

"I'm tired of it, that's why I moved into the woods."

"You moved into the woods?" I said.

"Yeah, deep in the woods of West Virginia."

"How's that?"

"It's beautiful. I live a peaceful life there, free from television, microwaves, computers, and religion. I'm free of everything technological and oppressive."

"Why don't you like civilization?"

"Civilization is war, a race, a battle for power. People are run by two things, jealousy and power," he said.

"You have a point there."

"People are primitive and too monkeylike. I can't stand them, and I can't stand myself either while I'm with them. They make me turn into an insane monster, that's what civilized people do to each other, they turn each other into monsters."

"I feel like a monster a lot."

"That's why I went to the mountains, I had to escape their madness. It's repulsive living in civilization. I didn't leave my cabin for a year, and then I decided to leave to go see my mother in Ohio. And I find out there's a war going on. It's disgusting!"

"You don't believe in the war?" I asked.

"No, I don't. I'm a pacifist. I believe all problems can be solved without violence. There is no need for violence. People react much better to peace."

"But war is part of being human. Violence is natural."

"Violence might be natural, but that doesn't mean we need it," he said.

"Perhaps we do need it."

"If we do need it, I'm glad I live in the woods."

"You're probably right. I wish I lived in the woods. Can I come with you back to West Virginia?"

"No, people are annoying."

"What happened to you to make you think this way about the world?"

"I was in Vietnam in the infantry. I killed a lot of people, a lot of innocent people."

"How many do you think you killed?"

"Over a hundred. I have to live my whole life knowing I took over a hundred lives away from people that deserved them just as much as I do."

"That sucks."

"No shit it sucks! I took orders to kill people, I could have said no, but I didn't, I said yes sir, and did it. I killed and while I did it I liked it. Then years later while I was driving my car I realized it, I realized that I killed people, that I took people's lives. Then I became depressed for several years. No one understood it; I was such a happy person. Then I became religious but that didn't help, so I bought a piece of land in West Virginia, and I've remained there ever since. Except for once a year I go and visit my mother."

"I can see why you're a pacifist."

"I have good reason to be."

"I think it's wrong how the government gets young boys to join the military right after high school. Those kids are so dumb and naïve. It's like the government is taking advantage of them."

"I was once one of those young stupid boys. I was so dumb, I thought I was doing it for freedom; I wasn't doing anything for freedom. I fought for rich people that I would never meet. I should've become a hippy and protested. But instead I beat up hippies; I didn't know what the hell was going on. I was sure that what I was doing was right, but it was wrong, it was cruel and wrong."

"I'm sorry you have to live with that."

"Listen to me kid, never go into the military. Read your books, go to college, have sex, but never go into the military, they'll brainwash you, and make you believe that fighting for America has meaning, it doesn't. Personally I would only fight if a nation was directly attacking America. If they were bombing Yellowstone, or the Rocky Mountains, then I'd fight. But not for oil, fuck no!"

"You think this war all comes down to oil?"

"Listen there are African and Latin American countries that have horrible tyrants just like Saddam and we aren't fighting them. So why should we pick on Iraq. I feel that unless we take care of all the countries that have tyrants, we shouldn't take care of any," he said.

"Yeah, but those countries don't have oil."

"You're right, they don't have anything we need. Well I have to go."

"See ya later."

He gets up and pays and then walks out.

I go back to reading.

I don't know what to make of what he said.

I guess an opinion on war would be most credible from someone that actually fought in a war.

I have no idea what war is.

All I know is that it doesn't sound fun.

I drink my coffee and smoke cigarettes.

A half an hour till war.

I feel like I should be sitting next to a television watching the speculations and reports, but I don't want to be home with my family listening to their speculations.

Everyone has an opinion, and I don't want to hear any of them.

Jimmy comes in and sits down next to me.

"Here again?" Jimmy said.

"Of course," I said.

"I sat in the park all day."

"How was that?"

"Peacefully full of turmoil."

"The war is going to start soon."

"Soon we will all be dead," Jimmy said. "Are the terrorists coming?"

"Why wouldn't they, if I were them I would."

"Maybe they'll bomb Denny's."

"They should, America revolves around this Denny's," I said.

"America hates Denny's."

"Of course they hate Denny's, Denny's is designed for poor people."

"And poor people are expendable."

"That's why they got mad about September Eleventh, because so many rich people died."

"And rich people shouldn't die."

"Should we become rich?" I said.

"Of course, it's the American dream."

"I'm the American dream."

"You surely are."

"I'm like Donald Trump."

"I know, you're a millionaire."

"I have millions, that's why I go to Denny's."

"Me too, I own oil wells in the Middle East," Jimmy said.

"I don't like this."

"Don't like what."

"This war."

"No one does."

"But we're saving a nation of people from a tyrant."

"But that's not our country," Jimmy said.

"So they should save themselves."

"Yes."

"But why shouldn't we save them?"

"I don't see why we shouldn't."

"Are you serious?"

"Yes."

"I thought you were against the war," I said.

"I'm confused, I don't see why we should, and why we shouldn't."

"I'm confused too."

"We can be confused together."

"As we sit here and drink coffee."

"And smoke cigarettes."

"We can be confused," I said.

"Yes."

"I don't see any clear answers to any of my questions."

"One will never get clear answers when it involves the actions of the government," Jimmy said.

"The war is starting, it's eight o'clock."

"You're right, it is."

"Bombs have just been fired."

"Soon people will die," Jimmy said.

"And they will never get to live another day of life. They will never get to fuck again or get drunk with their friends."

"They have to die, so we can drive our cars."

"Maybe I would rather ride a bicycle than have people die."

"No you wouldn't, you'd rather have them die," Jimmy said.

"You're probably right."

"Who knows, maybe you would rather ride a bike."

"I can't bear this."

"It's bearable."

"I know, and that's what is painful," I said.

"There will be a lot of pain in upcoming weeks."

"I feel so powerless and frustrated."

"You are powerless."

"Each man must learn he is powerless one day."

"And a painful day that is," Jimmy said.

"I'm a human, I should be able to do something."

"There is nothing you can do, except be pissed."

"What if I light myself on fire like the Buddhist did in Vietnam?"

"You'll be on the news, but that's about all."

"The war will go on."

"The machine has started, now it won't end till it's over."

"The machine is unbreakable."

"The machine has been working strong for thousands of years, it won't end for you."

"What if I pray for a really long time?"

"Prayer doesn't help anyone, you know that."

"I feel so powerless, so small, so worthless," I said.

"You are powerless, small, and worthless."

"Tonight I'm going to get drunk and hopefully forget that I'm human."

"You should try that, it'll be good for you."

"I will, I'll get drunk."

"And what will you do then?"

"Go home and hang myself."

"Why would you do that?"

"Because I no longer want to live in a world where bastards wage war on each other."

"The bastards have to wage war, it's what they do. See, kids who want to be soldiers do it because they are warlike beasts; they have to fight to feel human."

"But civilians are getting killed."

"They will go to Allah," Jimmy said.

"What if there's no God?"

"Then they go nowhere."

"They disappear?"

"Yes."

"I don't want to die."

"Personally I don't think anyone does."

"Why do we do it then?" I said.

"Because we have to."

"I refuse."

"You don't have much choice."

"I should have a choice, I'm a free individual."

"We all die."

"What if there's no God?"

"Then nowhere."

"All my memories gone."

"Memories gone."

"But my memories make me who I am."

"Then you won't be anyone."

"I always want to be someone."

"Well, one day you won't be anyone."

"What will I do that day?"

"Nothing."

"Forever?"

"Yes, forever."

"There must be another option?"

"It's not even an option, it's an ultimatum," Jimmy said.

"I like imminent things."

"No one does."

"We should wage a war against death."

"We did, it's called religion."

"I thought religion was to make sure people hated homosexuals."

"No, it's a battle against death."

"Oh yes, if you believe in Jesus you will have everlasting life."

"See?"

"I see."

"So if you believe in Jesus, you shall have everlasting joy in heaven."

"What if Jesus was just a regular man just like you and me?"

"Then it's not true," Jimmy said.

"Then for the last two thousand years people have been believing in a dumb guy who might have not even existed?"

"Possibly."

"Oh, this is maddening."

"Yes, it is."

"Could it be any worse?" I said.

"Probably not."

"Only if people knew that their lives were based off of bullshit, they don't know how bad the shit really is."

"No they don't, and they don't want to know, so don't tell them. They don't need to know."

"Will they ever figure it out?"

"Slowly they figure everything out."

"How long do we have to wait?" I said.

"Another thousand years if we don't blow each other up by then."

"I don't want to be blown up."

"It doesn't matter when you die, after you die the same thing will happen no matter when you die. Either heaven or nothing."

"I prefer heaven."

"We all do."

"Heaven sounds like a fairy tale though."

"I know, that's why it's absurd," Jimmy said.

"So all I am is a man on a rock, living a meaningless life, doing meaningless things, for meaningless reasons."

"Most likely."

"I don't want to be human any more."

"No one does."

"But I've had experiences with ghosts, what does that mean?"

"Who knows?"

"You're right, who knows."

"Probably even the ghosts live a meaningless existence."

"It must be hard being a ghost, sitting around all day in the same building, that must get boring and a little tedious."

"It has to be, I'd never want to be a ghost."

"When I die, there better be heaven, because I want an answer for this."

"Maybe heaven doesn't have an answer, and if they did, maybe you wouldn't accept it."

"If I'm in heaven, I have to accept everything."

"Why would you have to. There is always a chance for rebellion."

"And I prefer to be a rebel."

"It is always better to be a rebel. Following kills." Jimmy said.

"Following is for mongrels."

"There is no fun in following, but there is no fun in leading either."

"There is only fun in going alone, it is always better to be self-reliant."

"Self-reliance is the key to genius."

"Self-reliance is also the key to loneliness," I said.

"A long time from now we'll remember this day and not smile."

"No we won't."

Absurdity.

We sat in silence for several minutes.

The war has started.

I want a relationship, but it's hard.

Everyone who wants to go out with me is insane.

I can never find a sane girl.

Not that I want one.

I had one girl about a month ago.

She was in love with me too much.

She thought I was so smart and beautiful.

A lot more than I actually am.

I don't know what makes a certain person fall in love with another person.

My bet would be loneliness.

Most relationships I see the two people in them don't have anything to do with each other. They just think each other are cute, so they begin a relationship.

I can't stand that.

But I guess there's more than that.

There's connection.

Like you have good conversation.

But I don't even see that in relationships.

I see a horny man and a woman who doesn't want to be alone.

There is so much sadness in this world.

Nobody wants to be alone.

So we thrust ourselves into relationships because of reasons we don't even know.

But no one really knows the reasons why individuals do things.

Madness would be my guess.

I hang out with Kendra because we have good conversations together.

And she is really good in bed.

I don't know which one brings me back.

Most likely both equally.

I will always walk the earth loving Kendra.

I can't imagine loving anyone else but her.

I've loved her for so long.

Seven years.

We have so many memories together.

I would have to kill them all to go on.

And live a proper life.

I'm incapable of living a proper life.

Or showing real love again.

To anyone.

I used to say I love you with such sincere intentions to Kendra.

But those days are past.

Those days of happiness are over.

Now I'm left with the future and myself.

Absurdity.

"Jimmy, I spend all my money on sin," I said.

"Where else should it go?" Jimmy said.

"It seems like the poorer I am, the more I spend my money on vice."

"I thought you were broke, how do you have money to spend?"

"I got my income tax check."

"That's horrible to give to a broke person."

"Yeah, I know," I said.

"What did you spend it on?"

"Nothing yet, but I plan on going to the strip joint and getting drunk at the bar. I figure it'll cost me like sixty dollars."

"Yeah, that sounds about right."

"But I know I shouldn't, I should save the money for better things."

"Who cares about saving the money, you need sin, you're poor."

"I need sin to feel happy, to feel better about myself and this world."

"Sin is always good for that."

"You want to come with me to the strip joint?"

"Yeah, I'll go, I just got my income tax check too."

"Cool, then I don't have to sit there alone."

"Personally I love strippers. You can get touched by a woman without having to ask her out, or take her out on a date."

"Yeah, that's why I go too."

"Don't tell anyone, but I like sin too."

"What sins do you like?"

"I like pills," Jimmy said.

"Uppers or downers?"

"Uppers, of course."

"How's that working for you?"

"Great, I have a three point eight in school."

"That does sound perfect."

"Damn straight."

"I like alcohol and strippers."

"When we were little children all we needed for happiness was to play hide and go seek, now we have to jam stimulants into us just to get through the day."

"I know, it's horrible," I said.

"But that's what it means to be human."

"To be addicted to things."

"Yes."

"I don't like being addicted to things, but I have to be, I must be."

"We are all compelled to madness."

"I hate being compelled, it's like I have no control over myself."

"What use is it to have control over one's self, that's so boring."

"And neither of us want to be boring," I said.

"Being boring is premature death."

"My brother is boring, he's Christian Republican, he goes to work and plays golf, that's all."

"See, that's a horrible existence. I hope I always live an exciting life full of intellectual discovery," Jimmy said.

"I hope I don't die."

"You still worried about death."

"Of course I'm still worried about death."

"Don't be, it's not that big of a deal."

"I think it is."

"You think wrong, everything dies, it's the natural order of things."

"Once on television I watched an alligator kill a zebra, it seemed horrible, but it's the most natural thing there is."

"Maybe it's natural that we are killing people in Iraq."

"Maybe it is," I said.

"What is natural?"

"Anything that is biological."

"Is war biological."

"Aggression is biological, so I don't see why war isn't."

"War is natural then, so are we for or against the war?" Jimmy said.

"I suppose we're still against it," I said.

"Life is a war, this is just on a bigger scale."

"Perhaps."

"Maybe we should enlist."

"I don't think so.

"Why not, we could get to kill some Arabs."

"Well, when you put it like that."

"Yeah, it would be great, you and I out there in the desert getting shot at, shooting at people, killing them dead. Then staring at their dead bodies in the sand. Oh, it would be great."

"Yeah, that sounds so fun, killing people and looking at them dead lying in the sand."

"Oh we would have a great time," Jimmy said.

"I think we should give an oil well to each of the families of the soldiers who die."

"Yeah, because those are the people who really deserve it, because they gave birth to a child who died for already rich people to get richer."

"And I also think after the regime is gone, they should make me president of Iraq."

"You would make a great president."

"I know I would."

"What is your platform for Iraq?"

"I would create the biggest military in the world and attack America."

"Good platform," Jimmy said.

"I believe I can crush them."

"So do I."

"Then I would take over the world, and pillage it of its resources."

"Another good idea."

"I would rage against anyone that said anything bad about me. I would paint the world red with blood."

"Man, you would make a great president."

"I know, it would be great. I think I'm going to call the White House tomorrow and ask them about it."

"You should, I bet they'll let you do it."

"Of course, who else would be qualified for the position."

"You, who else."

"Will you be my vice president?" I said.

"I'd rather be the head general of the army."

"Oh, even better. I won't have a vice president, who needs one."

"You certainly don't."

"I want to take over China and enslave them."

"That would be great, Americans would never have to do work again."

"There's enough of them to fill every occupation in America and Iraq, no one would have to work again."

"You're a political genius."

"I've studied a lot of Jefferson, that's where I get it from."

"I can see."

"If I took over America, I'd nuke West Virginia."

"Why?"

"It's a useless place, it doesn't need to be there any more."

"Yeah, we don't need West Virginia," Jimmy said.

"Then I would put the White House in California."

"Good idea, can I stay there in the Lincoln Bedroom?"

"Oh yeah, of course."

"Can I wipe my ass with a painting of Bush and Nixon?"

"No doubt, I wouldn't have it any other way."

"Beautiful."

"Do you want to go to the strip joint now?"

"Yes, that sounds perfect," Jimmy said.

We stand up and pay for our coffees.

The war has already started.

Planes are flying over Baghdad.

To throw bombs onto the city.

Buildings will soon be gone.

Toppled.

Screams will soon be heard.

Then they will go silent.

There will be mass death.

Americans will be glued to the television.

Parents of soldiers will sit home worried.

Young infantry soldiers sit more worried.

There will be a lot of tears shed in the next few weeks.

I wonder if I will cry.

I hope not.

Death.

And then there was war.

I don't want this.

No.

I reject it.

I refuse to accept the world is like this.

But it is.

It's horrible.

And mad.

I do not know how to confront the day.

With this insanity.

I wish I were a child playing in the yard.

Or an old man sitting in a wheel chair.

But I'm not.

I'm young and I have to live with the memory of this for a long time.

How long will my life be.

Too long.

America has just begun to fight.

The clocks are burning.

Snakes are slithering through our hearts.

The animals are screaming in the wilderness.

There is no light here.

The prisoners are rioting.

The children are crying.

Christ is in heaven watching.

We all have scabies and we are scratching till we bleed.

Ulcers are hurting.

The sun is setting.

Lions stop hunting.

The moon is hidden behind the clouds.

There's a dust storm blinding us.

When I grow old.

This day will be a blur.

And it might not even matter.

Perhaps this is insignificant.

Perhaps the Iraqis will love freedom.

Perhaps they won't.

They never asked for freedom.

I don't see why we have to give it to them.

Of course I don't see why we don't.

But all the middle-eastern countries are ruled by evil regimes.

Why save this one.

There are a lot of good questions that will never be answered.

Like we would believe the answers if they were told to us.

Someday I'll wake up and this will be over.

Until then I'll suffer.

I don't know why I suffer, I guess it's habit.

I no longer believe that there are solutions to the world's problems.

The world is controlled by humans.

And humans are an insane species.

They suffer from power.

I regret ever belonging to the human species.

It's trite and violent.

I would kill myself.

But I want to watch the insanity.

What will these crazy monkeys do next.

The human species is a train wreck.

They're all mangled and distorted.

They're all suffering from disorder of the mind.

And they're not very intelligent.

They have no desire to know anything.

And the ones that want to know.

Are so consumed with vanity they learn nothing.

I regret ever being an intellectual.

I'd rather be a mechanic.

Or something simple.

But I'm myself, and I know more than the next person.

I didn't choose this way of life.

It just happened that way.

By divine will or accident.

I don't know.

I don't believe in a way of life.

I don't think humans can follow any code of rules without fucking it up.

The Christian way.

The Taoist way.

The Buddhist way.

I don't believe in ways.

Humans are apes.

And apes can't follow ways.

They follow their instincts.

I used to believe in God.

And tried to live the Christian way.

But instead I followed my instincts.

Man is constantly at war with his instincts.

Man is constantly at war.

I used to believe in God.

But it faded.

As everything fades.

The saddest thing about existence.

Is that everything fades into the past.

The past is so remarkable.

In my past.

I failed kindergarten because I couldn't read.

I got into fights with schoolmates.

I scored touchdowns playing football.

I smoked weed.

Played in a band.
Had braces.
Got a root canal.
Had sex with a fat girl in a church.
Went to the mental ward.
Graduated from high school.
Lived in California and Oregon.
Went to Mexico and smoked meth.
All that lies in my past.
I was there for that.
That was me doing those things.
Now they're gone.
All part of the history of my existence.
And someday this will be part of my history on this planet.
There is much history in every person.
It's unbearable to think about.
We all live long lives.
Absurdity.
Jimmy and I get into our own cars.
The radio is announcing the beginning of the war.
We have already launched cruise missiles.
They are currently pelting Baghdad.
While I drive to the strip joint.
People are dying.
Buildings are being blown up.
Humans are scared.

American soldiers are celebrating because they hit their targets.

While I drive to the strip joint.

I'm happy.

There's no better place to take away a man's anguish.

I go to the strip joint every time I feel sad.

Even if I don't have money.

I go and get a lap-dance.

I get some young girl to rub her butt on my penis.

It makes me feel better about being human.

Some say it's immoral that I go to strip joints.

But I don't care.

Everyone needs a little immorality in their life.

The war has started.

I get to the strip joint and walk in.

It's a little shitty place.

There's a small bar.

Only two men are there.

One old guy with gray hair wearing a button-down T-shirt.

He looks like he's retired from Packard and has money to spend.

The other one is an old black guy.

He looks like he still works but has money to spend.

Jimmy and I sit down at the bar.

There's two girls circulating the bar.

One is a mixed girl named China.

She's a beautiful girl.

I think she does coke.

And there's an ugly white girl.

I think she's an alcoholic.

I don't know why anyone would let that ugly white girl dance for them.

She's fucking putrid.

The girl's dressing room door is open. I see a pretty white girl getting ready in there.

It looks like Jamie.

Could it be Jamie?

I used to love Jamie this time last year.

I was obsessed with her.

I even wrote a novella with her as the star.

She smells so good.

But she hasn't worked here in a while.

I was hoping she would be there.

She would take away all my suffering.

The girl walks out of the bathroom.

And it's not Jamie.

I wanted Jamie.

Jamie is so beautiful.

It's unreal.

I sit sad.

Absurdity.

"Jimmy, I feel like crying," I said.

"Why, you're at a strip joint, you should be happy."

"Because Jamie isn't here, I wanted Jamie. Where's Jamie I want to find her."

"Dude, why do you care about Jamie, she's a white trash whore."

"Because she was interesting, she was crazy, I love crazy girls."

"You need to stop dating crazy girls, all crazy girls do is fuck up your life."

"I don't care about my life, I want crazy girls," I said.

"You're sick."

"I'm not sick, I'm the pinnacle of Normalcy."

"No, you're sick and mad."

"You could be right."

"None of these girls are very attractive," Jimmy said.

"This is the shittiest strip joint in America, what do you expect?"

"I don't know, attractive girls."

"All the attractive girls work at the Babylon, you know that," I said.

"I know, but that place is expensive."

"If you want hot girls, you got to pay the cash. Supply and demand, you know."

"Yeah, who cares? China is still hot though."

"You know it."

I watch China dance for the old white guy.

The old white man loves it.

He smiles.

He knows there's a war.

We all do.

But the girls have to make money.

And the men have to get boners.

That is the law of the strip joint.

I always wanted to date a stripper.

I've come close a couple times.

But the girls never would.

That pisses me off.

I want to go out with a stripper.

I think it would be cool.

You know.

And it would never work.

Because I would be thinking about Dostoevsky.

And they would be thinking about coke.

But fuck it, who cares.

So I've never dated a stripper.

And I probably never will.

That's existence.

Jimmy is sitting next to me staring at the girl who's not Jamie swinging on the bar.

I look at the girl and don't care.

I want Jamie.

The girl is overweight anyway.

And she's really tall.

Which I despise in women.

I can't stand a woman to be above five foot five.

And she's like five nine.

Jimmy is enthralled though.

He probably has a boner.

I don't have a boner.

I want one though.

And I'm not leaving until I get one.

I got money and I want to spend it.

On perversion.

The song ends and the Jamie wannabe gets off the pole and comes over to me.

I stare at her as she walks over.

She stands before me a tall red-headed giant.

"Hi, my name's Star. What's your name?"

I don't want to give her my name, she's not Jamie.

"Mark."

"Would you like a dance?"

I think about it for a long second.

I really don't want this girl to dance for me.

I'm not even attracted to her.

Kendra is better looking than her.

When you go to the strip joint.

You're supposed to see girls hotter than the people you fuck.

"Yeah, I'll take a dance."

The song starts.

She begins bouncing her butt off my penis.

I'm not enjoying it.

I stare at China from across the room.

She's still trying to get money out of the old guy.

The red-headed girl turns around and shows me her breast.

Her nipples are pierced of course.

She rubs her breast in my face.

That was nice.

She does a bunch of other tricks to get me horny and get money out of me.

But they don't work.

I remain bored during the whole thing.

The song ends.

I give her a five.

She sits down next to me.

"So what do you do?" she said.

"I write," I said.

"What do you write about?"

"About what it means to be human."

"What does it mean to be human?" she said.

"I don't know."

"Then how do you write about it then?"

"I just write it."

"You just write it, that's it."

"Yes, I type, then it's all right there."

"Right there."

"Yes, right there."

"That's unbelievable."

"Yes, it can be at times."

"Do you have a real job?" she said.

"No, I'm unemployed."

"That sucks."

"What do you do in your spare time?"

"Raise my kids."

"Is that fun?" I said.

"No, it sucks."

"How old are they?"

"Not old enough."

"Do you beat your kids?"

"All the time."

"That's horrible for them."

"They don't care, they go right back to playing after I do it."

"Oh."

"Do you do coke?" she said.

"No."

"That sucks."

"Why?"

"Because I really want some."

"What kind of mother are you?"

"A bad one."

"I had a bad mother, kids never get over that shit," I said.

"I don't care, I'm not them," she said.

"You're right, you aren't them."

"I'm me, and I'm a stripper. I'm twenty-six years old. I've been a stripper since I was eighteen. I've done nothing with my life except for get pregnant. You think I want to be me?"

"I wouldn't want to be you."

"I've never done anything all my life, I don't paint, write, anything creative. I've never tried to be anything; I've never wanted to be anything but drunk. I'm doomed."

"It must be tough to be doomed."

"It ain't easy."

There are a lot of doomed people.

They can't escape themselves.

I'm not the one to save them.

It's each person versus the universe.

Most lose badly.

I stare at her pretty face.

And wish there was some way.

I could save it from the madness.

But I can't.

I can only save myself.

I'm not Jesus.

So I just let her be.

She gets up and goes over to Jimmy.

She dances for Jimmy.

Jimmy is very happy.

He loves redheads.

I sit there in my sadness.

The ugly girl comes over and asks me for a dance.

I say no.

She walks away.

I order another beer.

I drink it fast trying to get drunk.

China goes over and dances for the old black guy.

He puts his hands on her ass and rubs her bare butt cheeks.

I'm jealous.

I think about fucking China for a little bit.

Jimmy is still getting dances from the redhead.

I sit alone.

There's a war.

And I'm sitting in a strip joint.

I'm impatiently waiting for China.

All I want is a dance.

Then I can go to the bar and have a good time.

China finally comes over.

"Would you like a dance?" she said.

"Yes," I said.

She begins her dance.

I love her body touching mine.

I caress her butt the whole time.
My boner slowly rises.
She does the motions robotically.
I don't care, I want a boner.
She jabs her butt into my penis repeatedly.
My penis is at full length.
I love every second of it.
The song ends.
I ask her for another one.
She repeats the process.
My hardon remains.
While she dances for me.
I forget everything.
All my suffering is gone.
I have a total moment of peace.
Tranquility.
Serenity.
Harmony.
The dance is over and I'm left blue balled.
I give her ten dollars and she goes on her way.
I look over at Jimmy.
"I love being human," I said.
"Yeah, it's great."
"Let's get drunk."
"Okay."
We get the bartender to bring over shots.
We suck them down.

We sit smiling at each other.

We don't care about a damn thing in the world.

We order more beers.

"Remember September Eleventh?" I said.

"Yeah."

"I woke up and saw the towers destroyed on television."

"That's quite a thing to wake up to."

"No shit."

"I got drunk that day."

"I only remember the morning."

"I only remember the night," Jimmy said.

"I went to school that day. It was like chaos on campus. I couldn't believe it, America was attacked."

"I spent the night at the bar, I got so drunk, I remember pissing in the urinal crying for America."

"I cried that night too, I couldn't help it, I was scared," I said.

"You knew after that day, America would be changing."

"America has turned into an Arab-killing monster."

"I didn't want to be American any more after that day. I wanted to leave the country, but I never did, I stayed right here. Fighting the American war."

"Someday America will fall like Rome."

"America is Rome."

"Bush is Caligula," I said.

"I feel bad for those young kids fighting in this war. They don't know why they're there. They don't have a clue what's going on. It's not their fault they're not intelligent to not take orders."

"But that's who they are, they're people who take orders."

"I guess you're right."

"I'm happy that I'm in a strip joint at this moment. There's no better place to be for the beginning of a war."

"Yeah, it was a good idea to come here," Jimmy said.

"But I'm not happy to be alive at this moment. There's something disagreeable about being American and human at this moment."

"I feel really discontent. Like there's something I should be doing. Like taking part in an anti-war protest or being over there in Iraq killing people. I don't know which one, but I feel like I should be doing something instead of getting drunk in a strip joint. But this is all I can do to support my country."

"Maybe we should sing the Star Spangled Banner."

"Okay, let's do it."

"No, fuck it."

"Okay."

"Maybe we should pray."

"Okay, let's try it."

"How does one pray?" I said.

"Don't you have to believe in God to pray?"

"I don't think so."

"No, I'm pretty sure you do."

"Oh," I said.

"Well, what should we do?"

"Let's get more lap-dances for the troops."

"That's a great idea."

We sit there frowning.

The redhead and China come back over.

We get more dances.

We both get hardons again.

The girls walk away.

We sit there rotting.

As we get older we are slowly learning.

That we can never control our environment.

That we are powerless.

That no matter how hard we try.

Nothing will ever get accomplished.

But we're like all humans, and we keep on trying.

It's compulsive.

It's human to be human.

We are like all artists and we think that if we create the perfect piece of art, that suffering will stop, that the human war will end.

But it won't.

The human war is ceaseless.

As long as there are humans.

There will be war.

We don't get along.

That's why we drink.

Because we can't stand other humans.

Alcohol makes people tolerable.

Or very intolerable.

For violent drunks.

I think I'm going to spend the next couple of weeks drunk watching war coverage.

I'm going to sit drunk.

Watching the false reports.

And bullshit.

My friends will tell me I'm stupid for watching it.

But I won't care.

I'll watch anyway.

I will unwillingly succumb to the media.

Media.

Media.

Media!

The media controls us all.

Without the media there is no civilization.

Someday I will kill the media.

I'm going to kill it with a kitchen knife.

You watch.

It'll be historical.

Mark Swift kills the Media on November tenth two thousand twenty two.

Civilization will collapse.

The monkeys will break out of their cages at the local zoo and take us over.

Then there will be the monkey wars.

America will lose.

Because Russia will sell helicopters to the monkey warriors.

We will all die.

It'll be great.

Everyone dead.

Lying all over the place.

It'll stink.

But the monkeys won't care.

They won't even bury us.

They'll throw us all in the ocean.

And let us all rot.

Absurdity.

Jimmy and I head to the bar for crapieokie.

Crapieokie is karaoke but with drunk kids in their early twenties and late teens at a piece of shit bar in Youngstown.

In the car I listen to the war reports.

It sounds sinister.

Death.

Bombs dropping.

Blowing up.

Then rubble.

I wonder what my children will think of this war.

Bush is a madman.

He doesn't care about anyone.

Him and Nixon could be best friends.

America when will you vote for a decent person.

I'd like to ask America a lot of questions.

But I don't even think they know the answers anyway.

I get to the bar, and go in.

The bar is on a shitty back street.

I go into the bar and stare at all the freaks that go there.

All the outcasts from Youngstown and Warren go there.

Goth kids, punks, indie kids, painters, skateboarders, and musicians.

A bunch of shitfucks basically.

I go and sit at the bar.

I order a Black Velvet and Coke.

I sit there in my own world enjoying the view.

The war isn't on the television; it's some comedy show.

Everyone is laughing hysterically.

I'm in my own personal hell.

I rub my eyes and shed a tear.

And then Missy comes over and sits next to me.

Missy is this beautiful shorthaired brunette.

I love her dearly.

She's a painter and reads Rimbaud.

If she would allow me, I would marry her.

"What's up Mark?" Missy said.

"Oh, nothing, getting drunk," I said.

"That's all one can really do in this time of crisis."

"You got that right."

"But I don't want to talk about the war. I can't handle it."

"I can't handle it either."

"Today is my last day at work," Missy said.

"Why, what are you going to do for money?"

"I work for a makeup company. I sell makeup to old rich women for thirty dollars an hour."

"That sucks."

"No, it's all right."

"I hear you graduate this year. What are you going to do for the big job?"

"Nothing."

"Nothing?"

"Yeah, I don't care, I don't even know why I got the degree. It's a fucking painter degree what can I do with that?"

"Go to New York and be a star," I said.

"Fuck New York, I'd rather stay here and be a big fish in a little pond."

"But you'll never make the money you could in New York."

"I don't want New York, I like my life in Youngstown."

"I wish I could say the same thing."

"Why do you stay here?"

"Because I'm mad and poor."

"That's a good reason," Missy said.

"Someday I'll leave and become great."

"You probably will one day."

"Yeah, I'll be a superstar."

"Don't forget me."

"I won't."

I look at her face and imagine her in a white wedding dress walking down the aisle.

"I'm writing a screenplay about restaurant life. See, I've realized how our generation has deeply depended upon restaurants to make money," Missy said.

"Yeah, I've thought of that. I've worked at least ten restaurants and I'm only twenty-two. Our parents never worked at restaurants, they worked at the factories."

"Yeah, the restaurant is like our factory."

"There's also telemarketing, and door-to-door sales."

"Yeah, our generation has a completely different

world of work opportunity than even people fifteen years ago."

"Our generation doesn't have much opportunity at all."

"No, it doesn't Most of us have given up anyway. Look at this bar, these are all middle-class white kids, and most of them will never finish college, they will just work shitty jobs, and get drunk."

"I hate to say it, but that's me too."

"It's me too, but I'll have a college degree."

"This world doesn't want our generation."

"No, and we don't want this world," Missy said.

"The world will be polluted to hell, and over-populated when we get it."

"And the economy will be a piece of shit."

"I don't think the economy will ever rise again. And the Middle East will just get more and more fucked up. And the terrorism won't stop until we take our bases out of there, and leave them the fuck alone."

"No, we're fucked and that's all there is to it."

"And nobody even knows it."

"And no one even cares," Missy said.

"Hopefully we'll figure it out before it's too late."

"Hopefully. Well, I have to go tend the bar in the back. I'll see ya."

"See ya."

There she goes the woman I want to marry.

I sit alone again.

Facing the universe.

I drink another BV and Coke.

Tasha sits down next to me.

Tasha is a notorious slut.

I've had sex with her of course.

She has a big white ass.

That is so lovely.

She suffers from mental illness.

I had to visit her in the mental ward two weeks ago.

They should have given her shock treatments.

"How are you doing Mark?" Tasha said.

"I'M FREAKING OUT!"

"Why what's wrong sweetheart?"

"THE WAR!" I scream it for everyone to hear and look at me.

"I know it's killing me too."

"THAT MONGREL PRESIDENT, I'LL FUCKING KILL HIM!"

"Calm down, get ahold of yourself."

"I WILL NOT GET AHOLD OF ANYTHING!"

I order another BV and Coke.

"Mark it'll be all right."

"THERE'S A WAR ON, NOTHING IS ALL RIGHT!" I screamed again.

"Mark, settle the fuck down!"

"NO, I'M FREE AND I WANT MY OPINION TO BE HEARD!"

"You won't stop the war acting like this."

"FUCK THE WAR AND THAT FASCIST BUSH!" I'm still screaming.

"Listen you're drunk, I think you should stop drinking."

"I can't stop drinking, I have to suppress my anger somehow. I think I'm going to start a fight," I yell at the crowd in the bar. "Is anybody Republican in here, cos if you are, I'm gonna fucking kill you!"

Nobody responds, they just go on with their conversation.

"Come to the back of the bar with me, and have a seat. Okay."

She leads me to the back room of the bar where crapieokie takes place.

There are lazyboy chairs from the seventies in the back.

She sits me down.

I fall into the chair drunk.

I stare at the mongrels called humans.

I don't like them.

All of them are for the war.

All of them want my kind and me dead.

The dirty mongrels!

I notice that Tasha is wearing a sexy skirt.

I get the urge to fuck her.

Or punch her in the face.

I'm not sure which.

I get up and get another BV and Coke.

I walk around bumping into people screaming "STOP THE WAR MOTHERFUCKERS!!!"

Everybody just stares and laughs.

But I'm fucking serious.

It's not that I don't think the causes for the war are just or unjust.

I just don't want fucking war.

I tumble into Jimmy.

I grab him by his shirt.

"STOP THE FUCKING WAR JIMMY, STOP THE GODDAMN WAR!"

"I can't Mark, this is beyond our control," Jimmy said.

"NO, STOP THE FUCKING WAR!"

Then I stumble away.

I keep gulping my BV and Coke through the straw.

I can no longer control my environment or myself.

I have to find a ride home.

I walk over to a really stupid hot girl and whisper, "Can you help me?"

"Yeah, what do you need?"

"I need to stop the war."

"I can't help."

"No one can," I say pathetically.

I stumble on.

I go back to the bar and get another BV and Coke.

The war has started in my mind.

Bombs are crashing into my neurotransmitters.

George W. Bush is talking in my mind.

Spitting beautiful lies.

I'm so tired of lies.

I seek truth.

But there is none to be had.

I want to go to sleep.

Humans are such vile creatures.

They deserve this war.

They deserve to die.

They deserve to have their family members die in the sands of the Middle East.

They don't care about anyone, not even themselves.

I no longer want to be human.

I walk amongst them like they're animals.

Because they are.

Animals.

Complete and total mongrels.

Mongrels.

All of them.

I will wage a personal war against them all.

And they'll love it.

Humans love humans who hate other humans.

Like Kurt Cobain.

He made a living off of hating people.

I sit in my cushioned seat drunk staring at the people in the bar.

It's their fault this is happening.

It's everyone's fault.

We are all part of America and its world domination.

We have no choice but to take part in it.

We don't know any better.

Like a dog who shits on the carpet.

Oh no.

The world and its madness.

Music is blasting.

A thousand bad conversations are taking place.

I'm stuck in the middle taking it all in.

Drunk.

Wanting to be dead.

America.

I lay back my head and close my eyes.

The room is spinning.

The dead walk amongst me.

Poetry is heard in the distance.

I think I might die tonight.

Here in this seat.

I don't see why not.

What do I have to live for?

Fifty years of being a drunken loser.

Fuck it.

I'll die.

Fuck!

I can't die.

What's happening?

I'm surrounded by humans.

The filthy monkeys.

I notice Tasha's friend Nicole sitting near me.

She's cute.

With pink hair in pigtails.

Pierced eyebrow, nose, and tongue rings.

She turns me on.

She begins talking to me.

I don't understand what she's saying.

I want her to shut up.

She says the phrase, "Will you fuck me?"

I don't know what to do with that phrase.

It sounds inviting.

I hesitate for a moment.

I've never fucked during a war.

I say, "Yes, but I don't know if I can get it up."

She says, "All right."

"Can you drive me home, I'm drunk?" I said.

"Yeah, Emily will drive you home, and then I'll bring you back to my house."

"That sounds great," I said.

We stop talking.

Now I have to fuck someone.

That sounds terrifying.

This night is madness.

I think I have to go to the bathroom.

I stand up and wobble a little.

Then I slowly move towards the bathroom.

There are a lot of mongrels in the way.

I can't stand these people.

What are they doing in my way?

They shouldn't be there.

I finally make it to the bathroom.

I lock the door and crawl to the toilet.

I put my face in front of the bowl.

And then.

Vomit!

It comes out easy.

The world is collapsing down on me.

I can't stand the weight.

I don't need this.

I did this to myself, but I was compelled.

The last chunks of vomit come out pretty rough.

I think I might die in this bathroom.

And no one will ever find me.

Until I start stinking.

Then they'll open the door.

And find my dead body.

Rotting.

I stand up and head back out.

The people are still there making noise.

I can't stand noise at this point.

I think I'm in a blackout.

I probably won't remember this.

I sit back down.

And pass out.

There is silence in my mind.

I'm at the bottom of the Grand Canyon.

There are pretty clouds hovering in the sky.

The sun is out.

It's seventy degrees.

I'm sitting with two Tijuana prostitutes.

We're drinking margaritas.

I'm happy.

There's no war.

Everyone is at peace.

There's a God and he loves us.

Jesus is at another table with prostitutes of his own.

There's real hope here.

America doesn't exist.

Saddam Hussein went to counselling, and he's a good person now.

George W. Bush got a tutor and learned the alphabet.

I put my feet into the Colorado River.

It's cold, but peaceful.

I feel at home here at the bottom of the canyon with my two prostitutes.

I wake up fifteen minutes later.

Noise!

The universe is a bloody cunt.

I feel less drunk.

Which is good.

I go to the bathroom again.

In there.

I shit.

It's hard shitting while you're drunk.

Trying to wipe is really hard.

My reality is mangled and distorted.

And there's no way out of it.

I go outside.

And sit on the grass cross-legged.

I light a cigarette.

And stare at the stars in the sky.

But they give me no solace.

The really stupid hot girl comes out for a breath of fresh air.

She says, "Are you all right."

"Yeah, I'm fine, just a little drunk."

She sits down next to me.

"You look like you are going to cry, what's wrong?" she said.

"The war, it's tearing me up inside."

"Yeah, me too."

"It is?" I said.

"Yeah, I hope we get Saddam."

"What?"

"I want this war, Saddam is a horrible person. And Iraqis need to know what freedom feels like. It's pretty selfish for America to keep freedom to themselves, don't you think?"

"I guess."

"Well, I have to go back in. See ya."

I sit there confounded.

I don't know what to make of this war.

I don't know what I should do.

You know what, FUCK THIS WAR, FUCK BUSH, FUCK GOD, AND FUCK AMERICA.

I'll just be drunk.

THE DOOMED

In the local mental ward sat two humans.

Each lying on his bed.

David is fat and unattractive.

Jimmy is attractive and disturbed.

"Do I look ugly?" David asked.

"No, you look great," Jimmy said while reading a book.

"Because I think I look ugly."

"Why do you care so much?"

"Because I look ugly, do I look ugly?"

"Do you think you look ugly?" Jimmy said.

"I don't care what I think; I want to know what you think."

"I think you're a beautiful man."

"You do, really?"

"Yeah, you're a great looking man."

"But do you think I'm ugly?" David said.

"You believe in God, don't you? Do you think he thinks you're ugly?"

"I don't know, do you think God thinks I'm ugly?"

"I don't think he cares."

"Why wouldn't he care if I'm ugly or not?"

"Well, I would think he had more important things to dwell on."

"I don't know what he would dwell on besides my ugliness. Do you think I'm ugly?"

"No, I think you have a wonderful face. It's very symmetrical."

"You think?" David said.

"Oh yeah, it's marvellous."

"My mother's dead."

"She is, how come?"

"Her heart stopped beating."

"That must have been tragic," Jimmy said while still reading.

"It was, she was my best friend."

"Your mother is watching you from heaven, that's what dead people do, they watch us, even in the shower. I won't even masturbate because I think dead people are watching. They watch all the time, every moment of the day, there's a dead person watching."

"My mother sees me lying here in the mental ward."

"Yeah, she's watching right now. She even watches when you shit."

"I don't want my mother to know I'm here."

"She knows, and she's crying a tear in heaven."

"Do you think I'm ugly? I don't want to be ugly."

David gets up and walks in front of Jimmy's bed.

He stands there retarded and drunk like.

"No one does, it's horrible to be ugly. I'd rather be pretty than smart any day."

"You would?"

"Yes, of course. Why would anybody want to be smart, it's such a hassle, knowing and understanding things. Intelligence causes suffering, but being hot, that just gets you laid."

"I haven't been laid in three years," David said.

"That's sad, you should save up and go to a prostitute. They're very convenient."

"I would never do that, I believe in God."

"It's obvious God doesn't care about you, so I don't see why you wouldn't."

"But my mother would be watching."

"You're right, she would. Why don't you go to a bar and meet someone?"

"I get nervous around girls."

"I get horny around them."

"Do you think I'm ugly?"

"I don't trust my own thoughts, so I'm not going to answer that."

"Please answer?"

"No, I refuse. You answer it."

"I can't, I'm not you."

"No, you're not. But I no longer trust my own thoughts, my thoughts don't make sense any more, I'm always thinking something I don't want to be thinking, but I think I want to think. Then I think what I'm thinking is right and true, but then I think of something else that contradicts that, then I think some more, then I take pills and cry."

"Yeah, but do you think I'm ugly?"

"No, you're beautiful, seriously, sit down, you're making me nervous."

David goes back to his bed and lies down.

Jimmy keeps on reading.

"They put me on new pills," David said.

"How's that working out?"

"I'm nervous."

"So am I, but then I touched myself while thinking of the Rocky Mountains."

"Sometimes I touch myself."

"Good, don't tell me about it."

"I'm nervous."

"So am I, it's unbearable. I'll have to eat today, go to the bathroom, I'll probably shit, and then I'll have to wipe my ass. It's such a burden to exist. There's a lot a person has to do to get through the day, and I have no interest in doing any of it. Why can't I be left alone,

I don't want to wipe my ass, it's disgusting, don't you think it's grotesque."

"No, I enjoy it."

"Of course you would, you're fucking sick."

"I'm not sick, the doctor says I'm normal, but do you think I'm ugly?"

"I like the doctor, he gives me pills. Some people say depression is all in your head, but I'm like where else would it be, in your foot? People are delightfully annoying. Do you like people? Because I sure as hell don't."

David stands up on his bed and scratches his bulbous tummy.

"I'm fat; you think I'm fat?" David asked.

"No, you're like Adonis," Jimmy replied.

"I'm like Adonis?"

"Yes, you're a Greek god David."

Melissa walks into the room and sits down on the edge of Jimmy's bed.

She is short and attractive.

"I got out of bed today," Melissa said.

"You did, that's beautiful," Jimmy said.

"Yeah, I'm real proud of myself."

"You should never exalt yourself."

"The doctor says I should be proud."

"The doctor is a madman, he lies to small children."

"No he doesn't, he's an honest man," Melissa said.

"Don't believe him, he walks among the dogs."

"What dogs?" Melissa asked.

"The devil dogs of the black forest," Jimmy replied.

"I doubt the doctor ever goes near a forest, he lives in Youngstown."

"So does Jesus."

"Jesus doesn't live in Youngstown, he lives in heaven."

"No, Jesus is a crack addict named Tyrone who lives in the projects, he drives a Chevette instead of a donkey."

David is still standing on his bed.

I'm afraid," Melissa said.

"Of what?" Jimmy said.

"Of the day, the sun is out, there's light, maybe it's time for cigarette break. Ten minutes till cigarette break. I can't wait, I'm so excited."

"Do you think we'll ever get out of here?"

"Don't know, don't care. I don't want to go back out there, I'll have to get a job and function. In the mental ward, you don't have to function, it's great."

"I know, I like not functioning, it's peaceful," Jimmy said.

"We're wild humans, no one wants us out there."

"I had a job six months ago, I worked at Taco Bell."

"How'd that go?"

"The boss said I was doing a bad job, so I threw a taco at her head."

"Did it hit him or her?"

"No, it missed."

"That's sad."

"Do you think I'm ugly Melissa?" David said.

"No, you look good David," Melissa said.

"Do I really?" David said.

"Yeah, do you want to have sex?" Melissa said.

"Can we?" David asked.

"You're retarded Melissa," Jimmy said.

"Why, David needs to have sex, and I need sex to validate my existence. I haven't had sex in over a month," Melissa said.

"Why do you have to be such a whore?" Jimmy said.

"I'm not a whore; I'm a good girl."

"There are no good people," Jimmy said.

"My mother is a great person," Melissa said.

"Every time your mother comes in, she tells you you're fat."

"I love my mother."

"Your mother is evil, evil I say, evil!"

Melissa jumps on top of Jimmy and begins punching him.

Jimmy throws her off.

"Take that back!" Melissa yelled.

"Fine, your mother is not a crazy bitch; she's a completely normal human being."

"Thank you."

"There are cameras everywhere; they're watching you right now. Do you feel them, caressing your skin?" Jimmy said.

"You're paranoid, there aren't any cameras, it's all in your head Jimmy. You're a putrid little monster."

"I love you so much my balls hurt."

"You love me, don't you? You want to have my babies, I know you do."

"I want to anally rape you."

"I knew it, you love me."

"I love our Lord and Savour. I'm married to Our Lady," Jimmy said.

"You're not married Jimmy, you're a loser, a loser!"

"No, I'm a winner actually. I graduated from college with a three point eight average. While you didn't even go to college, you sat around being a drunken whore while I worked my ass off."

"I couldn't go to college, I was too embarrassed."

"I want to hold you, come here."

"No, you're a buttfuck. You make me feel like a loser."

"You are a loser."

"I'm a good person."

"So is my asshole."

"I help the homeless."

"The homeless are drunk."

"Unlike you, I do nice things for people."

"You don't even listen when people talk!" Jimmy said.

"I'm listening to you right now."

"No you're not, you're waiting for your turn to talk."

"You're a fucking asshole, all day you sit in your room reading because you think you're better than us."

"I like to read and I don't like talking to people."

"You're talking to me now," Melissa said.

"Because you came in here, I'm obligated."

"Do you want me to leave?"

"I want you to love me, I want to share a house with you, I want to grow old with you."

"No, you don't. You just want to have sex with me."

"What's your point, as long as you're getting attention, you don't care."

"Shut up, why can't you be nice? You're always so mean and vulgar."

"Lick my nuts lollipop."

"Do you guys think I'm ugly?" David said.

"No, sit down; you're making me nervous," Melissa said.

David lies back down.

"My mother is dead," David said.

"We know, you've told us a million times. Get over it!" Melissa said.

"She's watching you David," Jimmy said.

"Shut up Jimmy, his mother is not watching him," Melissa said.

"I thought you believed in God, didn't you tell us all one day that he was coming back, and everyone but you were going to go to hell."

"He is coming back, and you're going to hell when he does Jimmy."

"Jesus isn't coming back, and I'm not going to hell," Jimmy said.

"Oh yes, you are. People like you go to hell."

"What kind of person am I?"

"A mean one."

"I'm a goddamn saint compared to you."

"I think you're possessed by devils, my pastor said that some people get possessed by devils and that's why they become mentally ill."

"I'm not possessed by shit, you're ridiculous."

"My pastor is right, everything he says is true," Melissa said.

"Your pastor is an idiot."

"You're a turd."

"You're a dirty monkey sinner."

"I'm not a monkey, God created me."

"God didn't create shit, even God knows that."

"God created the world in six days."

"God laid around and smoked weed for seven days."

"You're an evil monster Jimmy!"

"I'm pure of heart Melissa."

"Fuck you, I'm leaving!"

"Thank God!"

"Do you think I'm ugly?"

Jimmy, Melissa, David, and George are in the smoking room.

George is a man in his early thirties.

"I love smoking; it reminds me of the desert," Jimmy said.

"You've never been in the desert," Melissa said.

"I live in the desert, see that cactus," Jimmy said.

"What cactus?" George said while looking around.

"Do you guys think I'm ugly?" David said.

"Yes, David, you're a monster," Jimmy said.

"Are you serious?" David asked.

"He's kidding David, I find you very attractive," Melissa said.

"Quit leading him on!" Jimmy said.

"Shut up Jimmy, you're a mule cock fucker!" Melissa said.

"I took a shower today," George said.

"How was that?" Jimmy said.

"I think I forgot to turn on the hot water," George said.

"Beautiful," Jimmy said.

"I want to go home, but my parents don't like me," Melissa said.

"Don't go home then, go to the desert," Jimmy said.

"I'm already in the desert," Melissa said.

"Walking alone," Jimmy said.

"Yes, and forever," Melissa said.

"You can stay at my house," George said.

"You live in a group home," Melissa said.

"I do?" George said.

"George, what happened to you?" Jimmy asked.

"My mother raped me repeatedly when I was little," George said.

"That's horrible, you should kill her," Jimmy said.

"I tried when I got older, then they put me in the mental ward," George said.

"Where's my gun?" Melissa said.

"Why do you need a gun?" Jimmy said.

"So I could put George out of his misery. It's obvious that he's doomed," Melissa said.

"We're all doomed," Jimmy said.

"Yes, we are," Melissa said.

"Do you think we will ever see natural sunlight again?" George said.

"We would have to be let out for that to happen," Jimmy said.

"I'm leaving today, I know it," Melissa said.

"But where'll you go, you've pissed off everyone you've ever lived with," Jimmy said.

"I will walk to the desert."

"The desert is three thousand miles away."

"I have a good pair of shoes."

"My mother died, I saw her die, they pulled the plug, and there she lay, dead. My mother, my mother!" David said.

"Did your mother ever stick her finger in your asshole?" George asked.

"No," David said.

"I'm not dead," George said.

"No, you're not, you should be proud."

"I'm proud to be alive," Melissa said.

"You're also a whore," Jimmy said.

"I'm not a whore," Melissa said.

"How many people have you had sex with?" Jimmy asked.

"Around forty," Melissa responded.

"How old are you?" Jimmy asked.

"Twenty-one," Melissa said.

"You're a whore," Jimmy said.

"I'm not; I'm a good girl."

"You are the death of God," Jimmy said.

"Shut up, Jimmy. At least I've had sex," Melissa said.

"I've had sex, just with people I loved," Jimmy said.

"You're incapable of love; you don't have the ability to create bonds with people," Melissa said.

"I will one day, I know I will," Jimmy said.

"I was in love once, she weighed over three hundred pounds and had the most beautiful smile in the world," George said.

"What happened?" Jimmy said.

"I shot at her, so she left," George said calmly.

"Why the hell would you shoot at someone you loved?" Jimmy said.

"She was always eating my food," George said.

"Good reason," Jimmy said.

"My father shot at me once," Melissa said.

"How was that?" Jimmy asked.

"I cried for a long time," Melissa said.

"Sometimes I cry when I think of you Melissa," Jimmy said.

"Why would you cry for me?" Melissa asked.

"I cry because I feel sorry for you, because I love you," Jimmy said.

"You love me?"

"Yes, I do. I find you charming," Jimmy said.

"Ah. Maybe someday I'll give you a blowjob."

"I can only hope."

"I haven't had a blowjob in over three years. But I never liked them anyway," George said.

"I told the doctor I wanted to be free, so he gave me more medication," Jimmy said.

"Is it helping?" Melissa said.

"I don't want to be free any more," Jimmy said.

"What do you want to be now?" Melissa asked.

"Drunk."

"I was drunk when they brought me here. I drank a bottle of whisky, then I went to Denny's, and picked up everybody's cups in the smoking section and threw them at this picture on the wall of this one man walking alone in the desert. Then I got up on the counter and took off all my clothes. Then I think the cops took me here," Melissa said.

"What were you thinking about when you did it?" Jimmy said.

"I was thinking about the time my dad threw me into the wall for spilling a cup of Kool-Aid once," Melissa said.

"Why'd you take off your clothes?" Jimmy asked.

"I was going back to the primitive," Melissa said.

"One time I stayed out in the woods for three days, until my parents found me and sent me here," Jimmy said.

"One time when I saw my mother at the store and

she said hi to me, I went home and cut off my pinky toe. Look I have no pinky toe," George said.

"That's fucking grotesque," Jimmy said.

"You're deranged!" Melissa said.

"Do you guys think I'm ugly?" David said.

"Shut up monkey!" Jimmy said.

"No, you look good David," Melissa said.

"What do you think George?" David said.

"What, where, who, why, when?" George said.

"Do you think I'm ugly?" David said.

"I don't think about you David," George said.

"What do you think about George?" Jimmy said.

"Right now I'm thinking about when I went in the Marines, and I was doing push-ups. I had to do so many, it was unbearable. I was in Desert Storm, I killed people. It was horrifying. I think about those people a lot too. About their families, if they had kids, if they're in heaven or not. I think a lot about those men. I killed people," George said.

"Well, you had to do it. If you didn't do it, then Kuwait wouldn't be free," Jimmy said.

"What do I care about Kuwait, I didn't even know the country existed before they sent me there. And it sucked there too, it was completely impossible to find a prostitute there," George said.

"But you should be proud, you fought for America," Melissa said.

"I fought because they paid me," George said.

"I was little during Desert Storm; all I remember about it was those yellow ribbons everywhere. How come we aren't putting yellow ribbons for the soldiers who are going to fight in Iraq?" Jimmy said.

"Because no one believes in this war. I certainly don't, I'm a pacifist," Melissa said.

"You're also a whore," Jimmy said.

"A whore can be a pacifist," Melissa said.

"Only in America," Jimmy said.

"I killed people," George said.

"Do you think I'm ugly George?" David said.

"Shut up David, the only reason you say that is because you want attention. And no one is going to give it to you any more. So go fuck yourself you ugly piece of shit," Jimmy said.

"Fuck you Jimmy!" David said. Then he got up and ran out of the room crying.

"Thank God that piece of shit is gone," Jimmy said.

"You're fucking mean Jimmy; I'll never love you," Melissa said.

"I'm honest," Jimmy said.

"During high school I had sex with my best friend Joey Smith. He had a huge penis," George said.

"I've had sex with men too, there's nothing wrong with that," Jimmy said.

"I've had sex with over ten girls. I love the softness

of girls so much, but I love dick, and I can't leave it," Melissa said.

"You're absurd," Jimmy said.

"Shut up fag," Melissa said.

"How can I be a fag, and yet love you?"

"Because you're deranged!"

"I'm not deranged; I'm a normal well-adjusted individual," Jimmy said.

"I can hear you masturbating in your room, it makes me horny!" Melissa said.

"I do it for you."

"I think I love you too."

"When we leave here, do you want to drive to Las Vegas and get married?"

"Oh, that would be perfect."

"I got married once in Mexico to a prostitute. Her name was Leonore, she was a beautiful girl. She wanted to go to America, and work at a hotel as a maid. So we got married and came to America. We lived together for a while, and then she left after I pulled a knife on her and said I would kill her if she ever ate all the ham again," George said.

"You have a way with women George," Jimmy said.

"Did you ever have a relationship when you didn't try to kill the girl?" Melissa said.

"Once I was going out with this girl Jesse, she had the hugest tits. She left because one time she got really drunk and passed out, and when she woke up her asshole hurt like hell," George said.

"You're fucked up George," Jimmy said.

"I'm a Marine, semper fi," George said.

"I think I'm going to try to kill myself today," Melissa said.

"That sounds like a great idea. I tried yesterday with a shaving razor, but they caught me before I was done," Jimmy said.

"I've tried to kill myself eleven times, and I can't die. It's starting to get frustrating," Melissa said.

"I'll get my dad to bring his muzzleloader when he visits, you'll be dead for sure then."

"Yeah, I need a gun; a gun would do a great job."

"Guns are really good at killing people," Jimmy said.

"I killed people with a gun," George said.

"You shall not kill, that's a commandment," Jimmy said.

"I know, I'm going to hell. When I die, I shall meet the devil," George said.

"When I die, I shall meet Jesus," Jimmy said.

"Jesus wouldn't go anywhere near you, you dirty fiend," Melissa said.

"I'm holy," Jimmy said.

"You're impure, and retarded," Melissa said.

"I have walked the length of the desert to get to my Christ," Jimmy said.

"I want to die and never wake up. No more reality, no more, no more," Melissa said.

"We're just skeletons. Underground we will lie, while the world is still going on. Then one day civilization will be gone, then there will be no one to remember the great and horrible things humans have done," Jimmy said.

"Quit being so depressing. My doctor says we have to think positive," Melissa said.

"Yes, let's be optimistic," Jimmy said.

"Someday we will get out, and we will be able to achieve our dreams, and be great citizens of America."

"Yes, one day, life will be beautiful. Life will be worth living, and we will live it."

"At one point in my life I was sitting in the desert shooting at people I didn't know, for a reason I didn't know. At another point in my life my own mother was fondling my penis. At another point in my life I was married to a Mexican prostitute. And currently at this point in my life, I don't even know what day it is," George said.

LITTLE FLOWERS

My dad brought me to the train station.

It's a rainy night.

I've just graduated college with an English literature degree. I've never travelled in my life.

The farthest I've ever been from home was Virginia Beach.

I'm sitting in the train station in Youngstown Ohio reading. I look around the room and see a fat white trash woman eating Taco Bell. A Chinese girl and a white guy cuddling, and a lonely woman reading a romance novel. It's a sad sight.

It's two in the morning.

I've lived a stupid life. My college existence consisted of going to bars and sitting at Denny's till sunrise. I've had several girlfriends for long periods, but I don't know if I have loved any of them. I said I love you to them, but I probably just said it to get laid.

I've lived so many useless days. Days I can't even remember.

The train arrives.

Everybody stands up.

We all march out to the train and get in.

It's dark and everybody is sleeping.

A conductor takes my ticket, and I sit down.

I put my luggage up in the rack.

And lie down.

I'm nervous about this trip. I'm not one for adventure. I'm not one to live his life to the extreme. I'm boring; I graduated in four years, what kind of normal person does that.

I'm alone.

No one is here to help me.

No one is here to keep me safe.

I have to do this all by myself.

I've never done anything all by myself.

I'm not a loner.

I've always wanted to be a loner though. I've always wanted to be one of those guys that do insane things, have insane adventures, and just live a really cool life.

I guess this is my chance.

I fall asleep.

I wake up in the morning.

The train is moving towards Chicago.

I look around the train looking for somebody to ask where the lounge is.

There's an older man with a ponytail behind.

He has a stupid look on his face. But I ask anyway.

He answers, and then I go to the lounge.

I walk to the lounge and get a coffee.

I ask where the smoking section is.

The worker says there's no smoking on this train.

I'm very pissed.

So I go to the bathroom and smoke a cigarette.

It sucks smoking in a bathroom.

I realized I'm not at home any more.

I'm afraid of that fact.

I walk back to my seat.

Drink my coffee and stare out the window.

There's nothing out there.

Just ugly land.

I see a lonely cow in the distance.

The train arrives in Chicago. I get off the train into this huge train station. I don't know where I am. I don't know where to go. My reality is hard to comprehend.

I walk out of the train station after looking for the way out for ten minutes.

I stumble down the street looking for a coffee shop.

There are none.

So I go to Starbucks.

It's no smoking there.

I order a plain coffee and sit down with a book.

I read and sometimes look out the windows at passersby.

The coffee is too hot, and it tastes horrible.

The people of Chicago look pretentious.

They all look like poets and politicians.

I look homeless compared to them.

I finish my coffee and head back on the town.

I stop a taxi and take it to the library.

We ride around town for a little bit and he drops me off.

I walk up to the door.

And it's closed.

The taxi is gone.

I get another taxi and go back to the train station.

I don't know anything about Chicago.

I don't know where to go.

I don't feel safe just walking the streets aimlessly.

I'm afraid of missing my train.

Even though I have five more hours till I have to get on it.

I get back to the train station and eat.

I have a shitty cheeseburger.

Now I only have four more hours to go.

So I decide to get drunk.

I go to the bar and start drinking.

I drink rum and Cokes.

The world is slowly becoming a better place.

A young girl is sitting next to me.

She's pretty. She has short blonde hair, a nose ring, and tight clothes on. So I start up conversation.

"Hi, what's your name? I'm Arkady," I said.

"Hi, my name's Lucy," she said.

"How come you're at the train station?" I said.

"I'm going to New York."

"Wow, that's cool."

"I don't feel like flirting, let's talk," Lucy said.

"Talk about what?" I said.

"Your mother."

"My mother, why?"

"I'm not interesting in boring conversation," Lucy said.

"Okay, what do you want to know about her?"

"How did she treat you as a little kid?"

"She was at work most of the time, I never really saw her."

"Is she vulgar?"

"Yes, very vulgar."

"Does she fart in front of you?"

"Yes."

"Do you spend time with her now?"

"Well, I smoke with her in the morning at the kitchen table. We usually talk then."

"Do you tell her about your sex life?" Lucy said.

"Yes."

"I don't have a mother."

"You don't?"

"No."

"Why'd you want to hear about mine?"

"I like to try to imagine what it would be like to have a mother through other people's mothers."

"That's weird."

"I don't care if it is weird. I do it, all right."

We sit there for a minute in silence.

"Why are you going to New York?"

"To read poems at cafes. All I've ever wanted to do was read my poems at cafes. I don't care what job I have, it could be the shittiest job in the world, I just want to read my poems."

"That's a beautiful dream."

"You think, why are you travelling?"

"Because I just graduated college, and I want to see America."

"America ain't all it's cracked up to be."

"I don't know, I just want to do it."

"I guess you have a dream just like me."

"I guess I do," I said. "I'm going to just sit here and get drunk. That's my plan. What's yours?"

"I have to get on my train in fifteen minutes. I suppose I'll see you later."

She gets up and leaves.

I just sit here and drink.

A fat man with a beard sits next to me. He looks like a hick from somewhere out in the country.

"Hey kid," he said.

"Yeah, what do you need?" I said in a drunken voice.

"Ever hunt for bear?"

"Nope."

"I have, it's fun as hell. I shot one too, and killed it. They make great burgers."

"They do?"

"Yeah, they make great burgers."

"I killed five bunny rabbits with a pellet gun once."

"You did, how'd you do it?"

"I ran around the yard shooting them until they died. My neighbour paid me fifteen dollars to do it."

"That's cool. I should try killing a bear with a pellet gun."

"I don't think it would work."

"Neither do I."

"I used to kill birds too, one time I killed a rooster."

"A rooster? Why'd you kill a rooster?"

"It pissed me off."

"Yeah, my rooster pisses me off too."

Eventually I get on the train.

I'm drunk as hell.

The train is slightly crowded.

There's a fat woman talking about her well-adjusted grandkids.

I want her to shut up.

I talk to no one.

I've never been good at striking up small talk.

Actually I hate small talk.

I also hate people who talk small talk.

The lounge opens up.

They have two-dollar whiskey sours.

I run down there and buy one.

Then I go to the smoking section.

The smoking section is almost full.

There's every race of the world in it.

Mexicans, Whites, Asians, and African American.

We're all smoking for America.

A guy in his fifties wearing a beret covered with military pins is sitting in the corner of the smoking section. He keeps flirting with a Mexican girl who doesn't understand English.

The girl just sits there smiling.

I'm drunk and I don't care about anything.

I get up and walk around the car.

No one is paying attention to me.

I sit back down.

I start talking to an Asian woman next to me.

"Do you love yourself?" I said.

"No, I hate myself," she said.

"Why do you think about yourself so often then."

"Because I don't care about other people."

"Neither do I. I try to care, but I can't," I said.

"It's not worth caring too much about other people. You have to just let them go."

"I know, you can't change anybody, you can't make them happy, you can only piss them off."

"People aren't nice. I find them mean and ignorant," she said.

"I know, they're putrid animals."

"Humans are goofy and retarded."

"I don't know about humans. I'm one of them, and I don't know anything about them."

"Fuck it."

I stand up and go back to my seat. I sit there for a long time.

Years pass as I'm sitting there.

I eventually get up and go back to the lounge.

I wobble down the aisle.

I order another drink and sit at a table.

An old man sits near me.

He says, "Who are you?"

"I'm me."

"That's convenient."

"No, it's frustrating."

"Do you suffer?"

"Of course."

"Someday you'll die."

"I believe it," I said.

"There's no God."

"Perhaps."

The old man stops talking.

I drink my whiskey sour.

I'm exhausted.

I go to the smoking section for one last cigarette.

I sit down and look at all the putrid animals.

There's a girl my age with orange dreads.

I reach out and hold her hand.

She looks at me and smiles.

0207-361-3003
Ref# 04587/000334